Sweet Valentine

Miranda Maynard

This edition first published in paperback by
Michael Terence Publishing in 2022
www.mtp.agency

Copyright © 2022 Miranda Maynard

Miranda Maynard has asserted the right to be identified as
the author of this work in accordance with the
Copyright, Designs and Patents Act 1988

ISBN 9781800944206

No part of this publication may be reproduced, stored
in a retrieval system, or transmitted, in any form or
by any means, electronic, mechanical, photocopying,
recording or otherwise, without the prior
permission of the publisher

Cover image
Copyright © Evgeny Atamanenko
www.123rf.com

Cover design
Copyright © 2022 Michael Terence Publishing

Contents

My Valentine 1
Chapter 1: Debra's Boredom in Class 2
Chapter 2: Going to the Park 7
Chapter 3: The Photographs (The Final Break-up) 10
Chapter 4: Daydreaming Romanticisation 12
Chapter 5: CSE Maths 14
Chapter 6: Debra's Heart of Hearts 19
Chapter 7: The Shining Sun (Tomorrow a New Day) 23
Chapter 8: Mr Jenner Picks Up His Daughter 27
Chapter 9: The Sign (The Secret) 31
Chapter 10: The Last Lessons (Music Lessons) 33
Chapter 11: Drama Class 35
Chapter 12: Valentine Admirer 39
Chapter 13: Cohabitation (Love and Hatred) 41
Chapter 14: The Stolen Jewellery 45
Chapter 15: The Sufferer 47
Chapter 16: Marriage and Divorce 49
Chapter 17: Teenage Sweetheart 52
Chapter 18: Debra Skives Off School 54
Chapter 19: Valentine Reflection 57
Chapter 20: The Gift 60
Chapter 21: A Diary Entry 64
Chapter 22: Taunts and Teases 66
Chapter 23: Regrets and Disappointments 69
Epilogue: Paradise Dreams 71
Chapter 24: The New Terraced House 72
Debra's Memories 75
Debra's Last Time at School (Main Building) 76
Chapter 25: Days After School Ended 79
A Last Reflection on School 81

Any Valentine

On Valentine's Day, the romantic schoolgirls stayed together. They both engaged in deep Valentine's contemplation.

"It's Aldridge, isn't it?" guessed Claire.

"Wrong. It isn't," doubted Debra.

"Then who is it?" asked Claire.

"It's Coolidge," replied Debra.

"It is. Isn't it?"

"He's a sweet dumpling."

Debra and Claire walked away from another block. They head to another block where both pupils attended their next period. Both schoolgirls romanticise. They are obsessed with romance, as they both enjoy doing English Literature. The English Literature group set is full of avid readers and bright and intelligent pupils. They love the classics. They have a passion for reading romances. This classic they read today was a mystery.

Chapter 1:

Debra's Boredom in Class

During the Geography lesson, Deborah Jenner, known as Debra to her friends, talked to her schoolfellow. The school teacher realised Debra was not paying attention in class. The teacher called her out.

"Deborah, come over to the front. Come to the blackboard. Now, write on the board. *What is a jetty?*"

Debra obeyed the teacher. The pupil got up from her chair. Debra walked up to the blackboard. The teacher standing gave her a piece of chalk. The teacher stepped aside out of her way. Debra flicked her thick, wavy hair from her eyes. Debra stood still in front of the blackboard. She was nervous at being laughed at. She stayed calm. Debra concentrated on her train of thought. With the new piece of chalk, she wrote on the blackboard, her hand steady.

"It is a port…"

"Not quite right. Go and sit down."

Debra was embarrassed. She blushed. The self-conscious pupil walked down past the tables. She noticed the pupils' faces and their childish expressions. The pupil went back to her table. The pupil sat down. The English schoolgirl remained quiet throughout the rest of the geography lesson. Debra hated this period. Debra objected to how other schoolgirls talked and how they did not get into trouble for talking in class.

At the end of the lesson, the bell sounded. The class left the classroom. Going out of the geography classroom, Debra complained and grumbled,

"Look at them! They talk, don't they? But me, I get in trouble for it."

Claire tapped Debra lightly on her shoulder. Claire sympathised with Debra.

"Shush!"

Debra and Claire came out of the classroom. The schoolgirls both headed out into the corridor. They came across crowds of schoolchildren going out of the entrance of the block. There they both left each other. They went in different directions.

Suddenly outside there was a shower. It poured down with rain. The rain was heavy. Then it started to burst out with sunshine.

Debra went back into her form room in the History block. She stayed there. It was warmer inside than outside in the cold. The weather was bright and clear.

After registration, the form attended their next lesson. It was double P.E.

The schoolboys played football on the playing fields, while the schoolgirls played tennis on the tennis courts.

Debra wanted to see how Alex was getting on at

football. Debra desired Alex. Alex fancied Debra!

Alex played for the school team. Alex played badly today. He was on the losing team. Debra lost her tennis game. Her opponents were quite good at tennis.

Debra smashed the tennis balls out of the tennis court. She kept on missing the baseline every time. Debra tried her best at tennis. She made an effort to play the game.

At home, Debra rested in bed for hours. She rested until it was time for supper.

Debra did not do her homework as usual today. She took time off. She rested and relaxed. She was greatly relieved that it was the weekend tomorrow. She could have a lie-in until noon. She would recuperate.

On Saturday afternoon Debra looked at herself in the dressing table mirror in narcissism. She applied make-up. Debra looked really lovely. Her make-up accentuated her features.

She prepared herself for the party. From puberty, Debra grew up into a beautiful teenager. The pubescent schoolgirl was precocious, sophisticated and naïve.

Debra went to her friend's party. At that party, there were more girls than boys. Only brothers added to the small number already invited.

Debra was the most adored and loved teenager. She had a good personality. Debra was a really sweet girl.

At the party, her friends danced. The pop music blared out. Debra danced with her friends. Her friends were better at dancing than her.

Debra danced gracefully. Her movement was graceful.

Watching, the boys swooned and drooled over her. They had a crush on her. It was an infatuation obsessiveness.

Debra enjoyed the party. It was such great fun. Debra's hairstyle was so beautiful. A desiring beauty attractiveness!

Debra attracted attention. She wooed the boys there who desired her. They adored her. The boys revered her. Their submissiveness was boyish indeed. Adoring and admiring her. They loved her.

Debra had a good time at the party with her friends. Initially, her close friend Claire was not invited to the party. Finally, in the end, her friend Sandra invited Claire to the party. The gatecrasher invited.

***

On Halloween night, the children dressed in Halloween costumes in a Halloween procession which went from door to door in the neighbourhood.

Debra went to a Halloween do. There the children dressed up in Halloween costumes. The children wore scary masks. Inside the big room were witches, ghosts, ghouls, werewolves, skeletons and hooded cloaked figures.

Debra took off her mask and cloak. She wore casual

clothes underneath. She detested Halloween. She was of a religious conviction. It was against her Christian beliefs.

"You're a goody-goody!" they said.

With motive intention, Debra slipped away from everybody. Every person had not noticed her vanishing out of sight.

The Halloween night was eerie with a strong howling wind.

Leaving the haunted house, Debra got in a car parked outside the house. A friend's parent drove Debra home. Debra abhorred Halloween. The idolatry. The unholy glorification of it was a sin! The obsessiveness of committing a sin.

Chapter 2:

Going to the Park

Debra stood in front of the dressing table mirror. She brushed her long hair. Her fair hair was soft, silky and shiny. She had become narcissistic from her beauty. At that time, during puberty, it was a teenage narcissistic obsession.

Suddenly, Debra heard the sound of the doorbell chime. She put the brush down on the dressing table. She hurried down the stairs. She opened the front door. Her friend Claire came in. Debra was charmed by Claire's sweet smile.

Debra called out to her brother, "Are you ready? Come on. Let's get going."

Tim acknowledged in response, "I am coming."

Her brother came downstairs already dressed. They left the house together. From the residential neighbourhood, they walked to the park a short distance away. Going another way. They went through the entrance. They walked around the park. The park was quiet. They admired the beauty of the park. The peaceful surroundings. They walked past people taking their dogs for a walk.

"What are you going to do?" asked Claire.

"I don't know. Maybe I should be a model?" shrugged Debra.

"Everyone wants to be a model," tutted Claire.

"Do they? My mother has the qualities of being a model. I think I should follow suit, shouldn't I?"

"Well, why don't you have some photographs taken and send them off to a modelling agency?" suggested Claire.

"Yeah, I'll do that. That's a good idea. Just imagine me being on the front cover or in a magazine," said Debra dreamily.

"You ought to, you know. It's a shame you don't," encouraged Claire.

"My sister is vain," said Tim.

"No, I am not. It's natural vanity," blushed Debra.

Debra shook her long hair. It tumbled down beautifully. Her blonde hair cascaded.

Debra, Claire and her brother walked through the park. They went down to a quiet, shady spot. It was dark and shadowy there. There was a bench nearby. They sat down on the bench together in the open spaciousness. They relaxed together, enjoying the beauty of nature.

"Whatever you do, Debbie, best of luck. You're sexy. You take after your mother," said Claire.

"I really want to be a model. I want to do modelling," sighed Debra.

They headed off in another direction. Following the

path, taking a route to another entrance. Out of the park, they went the long way down through the park, making their way back to the house. This way back it was a longer route.

Alone together in Debra's bedroom, Debra played music. She put an LP on a turntable. Her favourite album. They listened to music. Debra played her favourite artist. Debra and Claire were emotionally impassioned and deliriously romantic while listening to music. They both loved the music playing.

Leaving Debra alone in her bedroom, her friend Claire left to go home. Claire took the bus home.

Debra did her homework. She finished it off.

Chapter 3:

THE PHOTOGRAPHS (THE FINAL BREAK-UP)

One day after school, Debra and Claire got the bus to Debra's house. Arriving at Debra's house, Claire showed Debra her photographs. They showed Claire's friends at a party. Debra recognised a few people's faces. Most of them she did not recognise and were unknown.

Claire usually showed Debra her photographs. Claire was deeply sentimental about them. Claire was emotionally attached to her sweetheart.

Claire showed Debra several photographs. Claire talked about every photograph briefly. Some of them were holiday photographs. At first, Claire had no wish to take any photographs. One of these holiday photographs showed tourists sightseeing. The sightseers were occupied with sightseeing.

Debra looked closely at these photographs.

"I really don't know these people," said Debra.

"These people are my family's friends."

"Who is the boy?" asked Debra.

"That's David. He's my sweetheart."

From that day on, Debra did not see any more photographs of David. Claire had broken up with

David. It ended up being a sad breakup.

Debra comforted and consoled her sad friend. Claire suffered from deep sadness, unhappiness and misery.

Debra embraced Claire before going. Claire was leaving to go home. Debra had deep sympathy for her friend. She sympathised.

Chapter 4:

DAYDREAMING ROMANTICISATION

In Debra's bedroom, Debra lay down on her bed in a relaxing, restful position while Claire sat on the armchair positioned opposite the bed.

"Do you fancy Liam?" asked Claire.

"No, I don't. I don't fancy anyone. In the past, I have received nice Christmas cards. I like the expensive ones. I dislike the cheap ones."

"Don't you fancy anyone?" repeated Claire.

"Me? No," replied Debra.

"They do fancy you, don't they?"

"Yes. They do. It's terrible. I don't encourage it."

"You will lose their love," said Claire disapprovingly.

Debra was unconcerned about being disliked.

"I don't care. I don't fancy them."

"Don't you fancy anyone?"

"Me? No. I have got my eyes on someone. It's more a liking, not a love!" admitted Debra.

"You do understand them, don't you?"

Debra had a deeper understanding of the opposite

sex, especially schoolboys who adored and desired her.

"Oh! Of course. I adore the adorable ones."

"Who's that, may I ask? Don't tell me. I think I might know."

Debra admitted her disappointment.

"It's disappointing. They don't come up to expectations. I have unfulfilled expectations."

"Not even one?" smirked Claire.

"I like Derek. He's a nice boy. He isn't my type. How about you?"

"No. I am not serious with anyone. I don't fancy anyone, not just yet. I don't think I will. It's pretty unlikely."

Debra shared her romantic inclinations about a schoolboy to whom she was attracted. She was captivated by an irresistible schoolboy in the fourth year at school.

Debra looked for Edward from time to time.

When they both heard footsteps coming upstairs, they changed the subject at once. They did not talk about boys again from the moment they were intruded on and imposed on by Debra's mother.

Claire decided to go home.

Alone again, Debra stayed and rested in her bedroom.

Chapter 5:

CSE Maths

After registration, the form attended their first period.

Debra did CSE maths. She was in the bottom set for mathematics. She hated maths. She was innumerate. She was embarrassed, frustrated and humiliated.

During the maths lesson, the class did algebra. Debra found it too hard. She didn't understand it. She was innumerate. Utterly bored, Debra twirled her finger around her flaxen strands of hair. Her forelock and fringe had fallen over her eyes, covering them completely.

Putting her elbow on the desk, she rested her chin on her palm. In a daydream, looking out of the large paned window, she romanticised while falling in love! Desiring the boys of her dreams. She desired love. She had fantasy desires. Her fantasies were romantic. Desiring and falling in love.

After the lesson had ended, Debra found Stewart outside the Science block, sitting down, eating his sandwich from his packed lunch.

"How was PE?" asked Debra.

"It was good. I was the fastest at sprint. I am starving," gobbled Stewart.

"How is your brother?" paused Debra. "Is he still singing?"

"Dillon is singing, but these days he's still singing out of tune."

"Tell him to keep up the practice," insisted Debra.

"I am tired. I want to go to bed," groaned Stewart.

"Why don't you go home?"

"I can't. I have to get the coach home," replied Stewart.

"I am lucky. My father picks me up, or I have to get the bus," said Debra.

Debra noticed Stewart ogling her. He was looking in her dark eyes at her thick eyelashes, her black mascara and her eyeshadow finely applied on her eyelids, her features beautifully accentuated prettily.

Stewart tightened up the strings on his duffle bag.

"Has anyone told you you're pretty?" said Stewart nervously.

Debra stood while putting her hands on her hips.

"Am I? Do you think so?"

"Yeah," grinned Stewart.

"You're such a charmer. I like you. You're nice!" said Debra sweetly.

Suddenly, the bell sounded. It was the end of break-time.

"I'll see you. I had better get going. My friend will be wondering where I am," said Debra impatiently.

Suddenly, the prefect opened the double doors of the main entrance. Stewart stretched out his arm to wave goodbye at a frantic pupil rushing in to get in the entrance with other pupils. Schoolchildren pushing in, pupils streaming as they squeezed in.

Debra attended her biology lesson. She was good at biology. This subject was such a fascination. Plants, human biology and anatomies. Her friend Claire was also proficient in the science subject.

The biology teacher told the biology class to prepare for revision for a test next week. This lesson was short in duration because of parents' evening. (Staff shortages may have been a factor. An indicative sign!)

Debra attended her next lesson. She enjoyed doing Spanish. Languages were among her favourite subjects. She spoke Spanish fluently. She was proficient in languages.

Debra missed Claire. Claire had gone to her dentist appointment.

In the Spanish lesson, Debra was quieter than usual. Her enthusiasm for the subject showed.

That afternoon her classmates did better than her. The Spanish teacher praised them for their good efforts.

During the Spanish lesson, they built up their new vocabulary. They learned new Spanish words. They had a test during the next lesson, despite raising objections.

During lunchtime, Debra ate her packed lunch in a full dining hall. That day some of her form had school dinners at lunchtime.

Much later, Debra skived off school for a specific reason. Debra had emotional problems with her father who had recently separated from her mother. (Debra also knew about certain pupils who played truant from school!)

During the night, Mr Jenner came to see his daughter at her home. She expected her father to come to see her. She expected worse things to happen. She knew of her parents' separation. She expected a divorce. This divorce was becoming more and more a likely outcome, hence divorce proceedings!

Mr Jenner came to see his daughter alone in her bedroom. He spent time with his daughter.

"What is it, Dad?" asked Daughter.

"I regret to tell you this. I am afraid it's all over between your mother and me. I am now staying at a friend's house. We are separated. We are getting a divorce. I am sorry I have to tell you these things. You do understand? I hope I've made it clear to you?" stated Father.

"That's a shame. I thought it was perfect between you two. Obviously not," groaned Debra.

Both father and daughter embraced a passionate embrace. Debra cried as soon as her father left her in a disturbed state. Debra was terribly distressed. Her emotions deeply affected her. She was emotionally unstable.

As expected, her father returned the next day. She approved of her father coming to see her. It pleased her.

He pleaded with his sad and disconsolate daughter not to give up on him. Continually, they should have this constant, deep love for one another. Neither of them should face desertion and abandonment.

Debra slept that night. She cried in her sleep. She was deeply sad about missing her father. The prospect of separation and divorce made her deeply upset, sad and miserable. Debra was aggrieved.

At the weekend, Debra stayed in her bedroom. She reflected on her father. Now her life had changed. The circumstances now were that of a single-parent family! How would Debra cope without her father? Debra desperately missed her father. She felt ambivalence again and again towards her father.

Chapter 6:

DEBRA'S HEART OF HEARTS

Debra waited at the request bus stop. She got the bus to Claire's house.

At Claire's home, Debra spent time alone with her best friend Claire. She spoke about what troubled her. She had anxieties, worries and problems. Her mind agitated her.

"My father is staying at a friend's. I am seeing less of my father nowadays. He can't stand my mother. They argue and quarrel. I can't stand it. I hate my dad at times. In fact, I hate them both. I thought parents were loving and caring. Not in the least. It's terrible. I can't go on like this. It's cracking me up. My friends have love. Their parents love them, unlike mine. Why does this have to happen to me? It's awful, really awful. My parents rant and rave. They shout the house down. These days, I stay at my aunt's. I get some peace at her house. My aunt loves me and cares for me. She cooks for me. I do like to eat her homemade grub. My aunt looks after me. She really does. I drink pop and tea. I eat lots of sweets and chocolates. I stay with my niece. She's little."

"How are you feeling?" asked Claire.

"Not good. It drives me mad, bloody mad! It drives

me up the warpath," replied Debra.

With consideration, Claire tended to be inviting and welcoming to guests at her home.

"You're welcome to stay here. Your mother is sympathetic," smiled Claire.

"Your mother cares about me. She is sympathetic," said Debra, touched.

Debra gazed passionately into Claire's brilliant brown eyes. She rested her hand on her friend's shoulder, desiring comfort from her friend. Claire was sympathetic, a sympathiser. Claire put her arm around her friend Debra, squeezing her passionately. It was a schoolgirl's love between them, a strong emotional passion. A strong bond of girls' love.

"We are around. Stay! We're here for you. Do remember this," whispered Claire.

They felt emotional love for one another. Claire consoled and comforted her friend.

Suddenly, Claire's brother William entered the room. They both felt uneasy by his intrusion. William was obtrusive. He intruded on them.

Claire left the room, leaving Debra alone with her brother. William wanted attention, intending to intrude on Debra.

"At last! We're alone," said William loudly.

"Oh, I am pleased to see you. It's been some time since I last saw you," said Debra joyously.

"Do you love me?"

"Of course, I love you. Why shouldn't I? You're immature. You have to do a lot of growing up."

"I like you. You're a good friend of my sister's," grinned William.

Debra was fond of William, respecting the teenager. Although William was stubborn and rebellious, she did like him. She had a really deep affection for him. She came forwards toward him. She kissed William affectionately on his cheek. Her lipstick was smeared.

"Be good!" exclaimed Debra sweetly.

William realised Debra was downcast. He sympathised.

"What's wrong? What's up with your dad?" asked William.

"My dad has separated. All this separation is driving me mad," answered Debra.

Debra was deeply upset. She tried not to get too upset about it.

"I do hope everything is alright," gasped William.

"I really do hope so."

"Oh blimey! What do parents know?" said William sardonically.

Losing interest in both of them and having enough of gossip, Debra decided to go home. Debra went home. Reaching home, she locked herself in her bedroom, wanting her privacy. Debra spent her time alone.

Lying on her bed in a comfortable position, her body positioned comfortably, her body stretched out, her graceful legs shapely, she began to cry in deep, childish emotion. Her tears ran down. She cried for the rest of the night. She preferred to be alone, away from her family, her depressive mother!

Alone at home, she cried in her bedroom, her silk pillow wet with her tears which trickled down. She was saddened at missing her father again. Her sadness affected her from time to time. She wept.

Chapter 7:

THE SHINING SUN (TOMORROW A NEW DAY)

Debra stayed at Claire's house. She avoided her mother. A depressive. She spent time with Claire and her younger brother William. William and Claire were sympathetic and respectful. They both listened to the sad teenager.

Debra expressed herself, "I can't stay at home. It's utterly miserable. There's no Dad anymore, just my bloody miserable mother. It gets on my nerves. Why do I put up with my mum? I can't put up with her anymore. Coming to your house makes me feel happy. It makes me feel better. Actually, being with friends who love me makes all the difference, you know. I don't want to leave, ever. I dread it, going back home."

"We understand don't we," said William sympathetically.

"We're here, so talk to us," simpered Claire.

"I can't talk to my mum. She just doesn't seem to understand," said Debra unhappily.

"You can talk to us. We understand," smiled Claire.

"Yeah, talk to us," insisted William.

Debra appreciated their deep understanding and

thoughtfulness.

"Thank you for being understanding and caring," said Debra appreciatively.

"We know your problem. We understand. Really, we do," sympathised Claire.

Debra felt so sad.

"I miss my dad. I am seeing less and less of him. He's got his life to live," groaned Debra.

"Isn't your mother understanding?" asked William.

"She's damned unsympathetic, she doesn't care."

"That's a shame. We understand you," said Claire.

"I know you both do," smiled Debra.

Debra whimpered. She suppressed her tears.

"All this grief. I can't stand them," moaned Debra.

Debra perspired as the sweltering sun shone through the windows. She dehydrated and sweltered. She was blinded by the blaze. The glare was blinding. The penetrating sun rays were a radiance. A blinding light. A resplendence. She closed her eyes. The sunlight and irradiance.

Debra came out of the room. She went upstairs. From the landing there she approached a bedroom while going past the corridor. She came into a big double bedroom. There an electric fan was rotating at maximum. The hot bedroom cooled down. Debra lay on the double bed. She had a peaceful rest and snooze that hot afternoon. In the shadowy coolness, she dreamt.

During the evening Debra and Claire ate their supper in the dining room at the dining table. Their mother made them homemade lasagne. An Italian recipe. A vegetarian dish. The lasagne tasted delicious. Mrs Watkins scraped the remains of the lasagne out of the dish. Mrs Watkins and her son ate the leftovers in the kitchen at the kitchen table.

"I wish I had a mother like yours," said Debra enviously.

"My mother wishes you were her daughter."

"Does she? Oh! How sweet!"

"She does," gestured Claire.

Debra spoke about her happiest times with her father.

"Spending Christmas with my dad was a thrill. A Christmas joy. How can I forget it? I can never. I had such a wonderful Christmas watching all those films at Christmastime. I, a film buff, watched countless films. The weepy, nostalgic ones, the black and white ones."

Debra remembered the nostalgia, her obsessive nostalgic sentimentality.

Claire beat her breast. "Do you remember that one? Come, My Baby Jane!"

"Yeah! Me Tarzan, I am Jane!" interposed Debra.

"You're funny. I remember those days."

"Make the tea. I'll be out in the garden."

Debra went out into the garden. She stayed out in the garden. The garden lights shone. It illuminated the garden.

Debra waited out in the garden. Claire brought the tea out in the garden. There, in the garden, William, Claire and Debra had a nice cup of tea. Debra was deeply sentimental about the romantic night. They all had a deep sentimentality in their outlook. It was their school's anniversary. They all drank their tea. They all stayed out in the garden until midnight before eventually going to bed at the late hours of the night.

Chapter 8:

MR JENNER PICKS UP HIS DAUGHTER

Debra got to school late today. She missed registration again. She attended her first period. It was mathematics. She did arithmetic. As soon as she had done some of her classwork, she stopped working. She daydreamed by looking out of the windows. She romanticised by falling deeply in love. She had romantic fantasies. Her dreams of desire. Her ecstasies of bliss!

After the lesson had ended, the pupil attended her next lesson, the period geography in the geography block.

Debra sat behind Kathy, a pretty schoolgirl, sitting at the front of the classroom. Her thick hair cascaded down her back. Her golden hair was brilliant in the resplendent sunshine.

During the lesson, the attentive class looked at maps on a grid. The pupils located a site on the map with its key which indicated the bottom of the map.

After the lesson, Debra stayed outside the Science block during break-time. Debra sat down and rested. She ate an apple. After the break, Debra attended Religious Studies. She learned about parables. She irradiated. She tried to fathom the ambiguous meanings of parables in the New Testament.

She attended her next lesson, technical drawing. This group was small. She used stationery during her Technical Drawing lesson. Debra was average in this subject. She did have a steady hand when using a compass on the paper, a large sheet of paper. The teacher gave her high marks on her homework.

During lunchtime, it poured down with rain. Debra stayed in her form room. She sat at the back of the classroom, near the warm radiator. She kept herself warm. She was seated on the chair. She nodded off in the far corner. Debra was unaware of her form coming in and out of the classroom.

After registration she attended Languages. She was quite good at languages.

After her lessons had ended, she went back to her form room in the History block with her form.

Making her way out of school, she found her father waiting for her in the car park. Debra was pleased her father had come. Debra was relieved that school had ended. She sighed with relief. Debra quickly got in the car. She felt pampered like a spoilt child.

Mr Jenner drove out of the school. The light brightened. There was an outburst of sunshine on that sunshiny and rainy day. A rainbow.

The car went past crowds of schoolchildren walking, their grey and black uniforms were rather beautiful. Going down the road, the schoolchildren were pedestrians. There, the lollipop lady guided the large groups of schoolchildren to cross over the busy road.

Mr Jenner drove his daughter home. Arriving home, Debra avoided her mother. She stayed in her bedroom until supper. Thereafter, she did her homework before going to bed.

She woke up the next morning before getting up to go to school.

***

On Thursday Mrs Jenner held up her daughter deliberately.

"Come here, love," said Mother affectionately.

Debra walked into her mother's outstretched arms. Her mother held her daughter tightly with passionate affection.

"I really do love you. You must understand. Listen to me. We have got each other. Don't forget our love."

Debra was overwhelmed with intense emotion.

Debra left her mother. She went to Becky's party. She re-joined Becky at her home. She apologised to Becky for being late. Her love was a conditional love, by the present she gave Becky.

Jane, Penny, Kate, Tina and Jenny greeted and welcomed her. She appreciated the welcomers' thoughtful love. She took joy from every friend's welcome. The greeting and high spirits were overwhelming, their welcoming inviting.

In a big room was non-stop dancing. Mostly everybody danced at the party. Debra joined in the dancing. Some of her friends danced much better than her. She tried to dance. She was filled with enthusiasm from dancing. They danced the remaining time. Those hours of the party. The dancing was so enjoyable and exciting. They had such great fun. The three tracks played were Sublime Trance. It was the best track played that night. The Trance music euphoria!

They were impassioned at dancing while listening to Trance. The dancing was incredibly thrilling and exciting. They were overexcited and euphoric. They did enjoy themselves.

As soon as the music came to an end, those that stayed behind and remained stopped dancing. The party ended. Becky was euphorically elated and ecstatic. She celebrated her birthday and engaged in birthday celebrations.

All of the guests dressing up at the party did have a delirious thrill!

The best-dressed one was a female. It was Katie! (Katherine, her proper name. It's Katherine with the 'k', not the 'c'.)

They embraced each other before saying goodbye. They were tearful and emotional at leaving Becky's birthday party. They were good friends.

Chapter 9:

The Sign (The Secret)

On Friday afternoon, Debra came home from school. She prepared herself for YP. She ate her dinner, took a shower and rested. She applied make-up. She looked lovelier. A gorgeous teenager!

On Friday evening, Debra was picked up and taken to YP. She attended YP. During YP they sang songs (songs from the Christian Week).

They praised and worshipped. Worshippers spoke in tongues. Debra did not understand it.

A prophet elder spoke out. He made a prophecy:

"My child, seek salvation. You are in darkness. You must see the light. You must turn away from darkness. And live in the light. The Lord thy God has plans for your life. You must repent. Seek redemption and follow the Lord. Believe in the Lord. Follow the Lord. Don't look back."

After YP Debra was invited to a back room. There, session musicians played: a guitarist and bassist, the sound of the music electrifyingly beautiful and melodic.

Alone with the band members, Debra cherished her privilege. She was overwhelmed at being privileged.

That night the session musicians played an

instrumental track. Their playing was unforgettable! Debra never forgot her memory. It was a memorable experience. She remembered it with great joy!

To this day, Debra told no one her secret. It remained a secret!

Chapter 10:

The Last Lessons (Music Lessons)

Debra went to secondary school in the afternoon. Expectedly, she met Irish Catherine in the Music block.

In the music room, her friend Laura played the piano while Catherine sang well. Debra was impressed at Catherine's singing.

Laura and Catherine stayed in the music room until it was time to leave. The music room was used for something else. This time it was used for music practice. A few fifth-year schoolgirls from a string quartet played well.

Leaving the music room, Debra and Catherine stood and talked outside the Music block. In one of the music rooms, the music teacher used it to mark pupils' homework and to prepare for the next lesson for the third-years. The other music room was used for rehearsals. The studio was soundproofed.

"How is your dad?" asked Catherine.

"Don't ask. My parents are separated. They are getting divorced," replied Debra.

"Oh! I am sorry to hear it."

"These days my father lives somewhere else. I still

live with my mum. Life's bloody awful!"

"Separation and divorce must be awful," said Catherine.

Debra refrained from saying anything else. Although she was deeply sad and upset, she still remained cheerful, buoyant and exuberant.

Catherine held out her hand. Debra took hold of her friend's hand. She squeezed Catherine's hand with affection, Debra was passionate.

"I'd like to help if I can," smiled Catherine.

"Yeah, me too. I'd like to help," said Laura.

After registration, Debra attended her music lessons. At double music, they sang songs. The music teacher sat and played the piano. The music lesson was electrifyingly exciting.

The music class rounded off school by singing in their double music lesson. The last lesson was a thrilling joy. The last period was memorable. Debra's memories come flooding back.

Chapter 11:

Drama Class

Debra skived off school during the morning. She went to school in the afternoon. During the afternoon, she went to the playground. There she found her schoolfellows from other classes (her schoolfellows belong to different forms).

Debra sat out in the playground. She sat with her friends on coats which were laid down on the concrete ground. There Debra sat with her friends at the far corner of the playground. There they had privacy without anyone intending to intrude on them. The outsiders left them alone. Other schoolchildren may have had mixed emotions. The schoolboys and schoolgirls were either happy or unhappy, troubled and indifferent. Some were peaceful, troubled and agitated. Debra was aggrieved and troubled. She had anxiety.

"Where were you?" asked Claire.

"I have just come in. Coming in for my last two lessons," said Debra calmly.

"What's the point? Is it worth it?" said Pete.

Debra's schoolfellow was a friend of Pete's. Pete remained standing as he had walked away the moment something else had distracted him.

The schoolgirls sat amongst themselves. They leaned against the fence. Debra, Claire, Rachel and Helen sat with their legs stretched out. Their sheer stockings gleamed in the light.

"What's happening with your dad?" asked Claire.

"My dad has moved out. He's staying at a friend's," replied Debra.

Helen noticed Debra's sad look.

"You look down. At least you have still got your mother," said Helen.

In joyful contemplation, Debra rejoiced, "My mum does love me!"

"The separation has affected you," said Rachel softly.

"I do dread the divorce, the effect it will have on me and my life," said Debra.

Debra was contemplative and philosophical in retrospect.

"I was once happy. Now I am sad about my parents' separation. My father moved out, living his new life. I dread to think of the divorce."

The schoolgirls observed everybody else. They caught sight of them smoking. The fifth years standing in a corner of the playground.

"They're smoking. It's now allowed," said Rachel.

"Are they?" they said.

"I don't smoke. It's a bad habit," scorned Debra.

"We smoke," said Helen unashamedly.

"We don't," said Debra concernedly.

"You're health-conscious," said Claire admiringly.

The schoolgirls sitting together had observed the smokers. They may have been corrupted by their observations. The sight of smoking.

The schoolboys played football in the playground. Moving about they were unaware of it. They were fit and energetic at playing football.

After lunchtime, the numerous schoolchildren left the playground. One of Debra's teachers was on playground duty. They went back to their form room.

Debra and Claire separated from Helen and Rachel, going different ways back to their form room. Debra attended registration. The attendance for registration was almost full (except for one absentee. That pupil went to the doctor's, her absence was explained in a letter).

Debra attended her next lessons. Double Drama. In a hall, the drama class gathered.

"Now, Debra and Peter can you come out to the front? Now, Debra, act. You're a virgin bride. Peter is your husband," said the drama teacher.

Debra acted. She was a bride in love! Debra acted while making her expressions of a bride madly in love!

Her husband Peter was deeply in love with his wife. Both Debra and Peter acted well in front of a camera on a tripod recording the romantic scene.

Those that stood watching were impressed by the acting. The romantic scene was deeply moving and touching. The emotional scene was filmed.

Everybody in the Drama department had seen it, Debra and Peter's brilliant acting.

Chapter 12:

Valentine Admirer

On one school day, Debra was wandering the school grounds. Debra was baffled by the group of schoolboys talking. She came up to the talkative and quiet schoolboys. She was quite positive that one of them was an admirer, a sender of a Valentine's card. She was surprised at the Valentine's surprise. She took an interest in Chris, appreciating his romantic love (her fantasies of love and desire a rapture and frenzy).

"Chris, are you my admirer?"

Chris blushed. "Don't be silly!"

"Is it you? Are you the admirer? Tell me. Is it a secret?"

Chris in embarrassment denied it. "It's not me. It's no secret," shrugged Chris.

"Well, if it isn't you, then who is it?"

Chris smirked and flushed.

"It's not me. It must be someone else."

Debra suspected the smirker as the secret admirer.

"It's you, isn't it?" accused Debra.

"It ain't me."

The baffled schoolboys wondered. They thought Valentine's Day was a secret romance, especially receiving Valentine's cards.

One of them spoke up.

"Valentine is a secret!"

"Yes, a secret love."

Debra walked away, heading to the main entrance, suspecting one of the older schoolboys was a secret admirer!

That night she looked at her beautiful Valentine's cards, wondering who her Valentine admirer was, her secret admirers! She was perplexed at her Valentine's love!

Debra was baffled at her different admirers. It could be anyone, any of the besotted admirers.

Chapter 13:

Cohabitation (Love and Hatred)

Mr Jenner showed his daughter his intended. Debra met Mrs Morgan at her home. Mr Jenner introduced his daughter to Mrs Morgan.

"It's nice to meet you. My father has told me so much about you," said Debra.

"I am pleased to meet you. You're the lovely daughter," greeted Mrs Morgan.

Mrs Morgan embraced Debra.

"I love your dad. I love him so much," said Mrs Morgan affectionately.

Debra stepped in the middle between them.

"How about Mum?" said Debra.

"Your mother has got her own life. It's over between us. You must stop living in the past, but look to the future," said Father frankly.

Mrs Morgan showed Debra around her five-bedroomed detached house. Full of envy and enthusiasm, Debra looked around every room, admiring the luxurious house. Debra did covet the house naturally.

"Yeah, it's nice. It has such lovely rooms," remarked Debra.

Debra took note of the following things: the décor, furniture, antiques, paintings, pictures and appliances, also the luxurious kitchen, lounge and bathroom too.

"Your father will be happy here, I am sure of it," said Mrs Morgan.

"What do you do for a profession?" asked Debra.

"Don't you know? I am a chartered accountant," replied Mrs Morgan.

"So, you do figures and accounts?" said Debra.

The sybarite curled up on the settee. From the table, Mrs Morgan took a box of chocolates and offered luxury chocolates to them. Both Debra and her father took chocolates. Debra indulged in milk chocolates. Debra found eating chocolates to be an aphrodisiac. She desired attention, love and affection from her neglectful father.

"Your father has moved in with me," said Mrs Morgan cheerfully.

"No more mother dear," teased Father.

Mr Jenner cohabited. Debra thought of her father as a cohabiter. She knew Mrs Morgan was a mistress, cohabiter and concubine.

Debra was flustered. Debra did accept the new changes in her life. Did she approve or disapprove?

"How's life right now?" asked Mrs Morgan.

"It's not good. I am having a miserable time. Life is such a misery," answered Debra.

"You're welcome here. You can stay," smiled Mrs Morgan.

"Yes, you can, dear," said Father.

Debra appreciated Mrs Morgan's welcome, and also the welcomer's offer. She was appreciative of the invitation!

"I would like to come here. It will make a change from where I am still living. Thank you for inviting me," said Debra appreciatively.

"I love your dad. You are most welcome here," said Mrs Morgan.

"If you get tired of your mother, do come," invited Father.

"How is your mom?" asked Mrs Morgan.

Debra was serious in her response. "My mom is really unhappy. She dreads the prospect of selling up the house. My mum hates you, Dad. She really does. I think of all our good times together, our good memories. Now it haunts me. My life is becoming unhappy. I don't like the changes. I dislike having to live in a small house. I hate the idea of it," said Debra seriously.

"That can't be helped. Things have to change," said Father.

Debra played with the toddler crawling on the carpet. Debra rattled a plaything. She did have childish ways.

Mrs Morgan brooded about having another baby. She desired a daughter.

Debra enjoyed the changes in her circumstances. She appreciated the invitation to Mrs Morgan's home.

Everything now was strange, new and different. The suburb was residential and middle-class, the suburbanites affluent.

Debra spoke no more to her father and lover Mrs Morgan. She left them both together alone. She stayed in a spare bedroom. Her bedroom was small and luxurious. She liked the cosy, beautiful house.

Debra ended up staying at Mrs Morgan's home. Debra was snug in bed, the white bedsheets fresh and clean. She rested after writing an essay for her English homework.

Chapter 14:

THE STOLEN JEWELLERY

Debra came home from Claire's house. She went upstairs to her bedroom. She moved to her dressing table. She found the lock of her jewellery box tampered with and broken, all of her jewels and jewellery stolen.

Debra retraced what she had last done with her precious diamond ring. She was certain she had put it in her jewellery box. The jewellery box was empty. Everything in it had been stolen. Debra was enraged.

In shock and fury, she came downstairs. She burst into the lounge. She questioned her mother.

"Have you taken my jewellery?" asked Debra.

"No, darling, I haven't taken it."

"It can't be my father. My father wouldn't do that."

"Where is your jewellery?"

"If you didn't take it, who did?"

Debra telephoned her father. She was angry.

"By the way, Dad, did you take my jewellery?"

"No, honey! I haven't!" answered Father.

"It's stolen," whimpered Debra.

"I have told you not to wear too much jewellery. You don't listen. Do make sure you're safe. Lock up. Stay safe!" warned Father.

***

On Monday, Claire came round to Debra's house. Debra had been absent from school today.

"Who did it?" asked Claire.

"I don't know," replied Debra.

"What was taken?" enquired Claire.

"I have lost the bloody lot."

Claire embraced her mad friend.

Debra calmed down from Claire's passionate squeeze of her body. Claire comforted Debra. Claire consoled her. Claire slipped a gold ring on Debra's finger.

"You can have this."

Debra appreciated her thoughtful friend's love.

With her right hand, Debra stretched out her fingers, admiring the gold ring for the first time.

Chapter 15:

The Sufferer

Debra was reluctant to go to school today. Her mother wrote her daughter an absence note.

Early in the morning, Debra waited at the school grounds until it was time to go. One member of her form teased her.

"You're a poor bitch!" insulted Lisa.

Those members of her form smirked and laughed. Debra blushed. She was humiliated and embarrassed.

Claire protected Debra.

"Leave her alone!" defended Claire.

Claire led Debra away from those in her form.

Attending registration, Debra gave in her absence note to her form tutor. It read:

Dear Sir,
My daughter was unable to go to school. Debra has had her jewellery stolen. Debra is suffering. Debra can't concentrate on her schoolwork. The theft is far too much for her to cope with. I have told her about the risks of wearing jewellery to school. Perhaps my stubborn daughter will take note of what I have to say. This is not the first time I have warned her.

Yours sincerely,

Mrs Jenner.

Debra couldn't cope. She was upset, miserable and deeply unhappy. With her school chum Claire leaving her alone, Debra felt vulnerable and exposed without her schoolfellow being present.

Making her way to her first period, Debra wandered away, going somewhere else. In the end, she skived off school. Her note covered her absence. The sufferer suffered in silence.

She took the bus back home. At home, she rocked herself in her bedroom. She cried.

After school, Claire went to Debra's house. Claire ended up staying an hour with her best friend. During that time Claire comforted and consoled Debra again.

Debra fretted, appreciating Claire comforting her. She felt much better from her friend's intimate love.

Debra skived off school all week. Not even her friends with deep concern and love could resolve the situation.

Getting back to school, her schoolfriends tried to offer her help and comfort as well as trying to console her.

Chapter 16:

Marriage and Divorce

Debra came home from school. Mrs Jenner told her daughter off for her disobedience and stubbornness.

"No parties. You're not going to another party. Get yourself a job. Get yourself a career. Stop wasting time. Stop fooling about."

Debra engaged in serious contemplation.

"I am serious. I am not fooling about."

"Your father lives his life," paused Mother. "Does he really care about you?"

"My dad does care. He invites me over."

"You will be poorer. You will live in a smaller house. Your father will get his half of the proceeds. He will live with his fancy woman," snarled Mother.

"My father can't stand you. He will live his own life. He will probably get married again."

"Who's going to take care of you?"

"My father will. I know he will. You certainly won't, will you, Mum?"

"Of course, I will. I love you. You're my sweet daughter," smiled Mother.

Debra held her mother. She squeezed her tightly.

"I love you, Mum," whispered her daughter.

"What's his woman like?" asked Mother.

"She's a businesswoman. She's kind and nice. She likes me. I think she approves of me."

"I can't stand life, this divorce settlement," moaned Mother.

"We have to move on. For the better or the worse. You have lost your husband. My dad will get married again. He will live in a fine house. He will live a fine life," murmured Daughter.

"At the expense of me!" glowered Mother.

"Getting a divorce is unpleasant. Life has changed. We are worse off financially. But at least we have peace now. That's the main thing. Peace, perfect peace."

"Our lives will never be the same again," groaned Mother.

"Some day, Mum, you will marry again."

"Honey, I don't know. I will never marry again.

"You will. You'll see. My dad will marry again!" predicted Daughter.

Debra thought of her friends' parents' marriages. Their good marriages.

Debra's parents' marriage ended up in divorce. Debra thought of her parents' marriage, how love broke down and the way it ended up in divorce.

Feeling upset, Mrs Jenner avoided her daughter. Debra did prefer to be all alone. Separating herself in isolation was a preference.

Her thoughts of divorce were upsetting to one's mind. Debra considered marriage a sensible and wise option. An alternative option.

Debra thought of how very upset and miserable her parents had been after the divorce. For her parents, it may have been the best thing for them in getting a divorce!

Hours later Claire came to Debra's house. Claire confided in Debra.

"Divorce is the best thing. That's what."

"I guess you are right. My parents can't go on like this. It just has to end," said Debra conclusively.

"Your parents have been married for ages. It is time for them to go separate ways," said Claire unsympathetically.

Chapter 17:

Teenage Sweetheart

Debra looked at old photographs with her unenthusiastic father. She took an enthusiastic interest in looking at every photograph.

The photographs showed Mr Jenner with his wife, both husband and wife deliriously joyful. At that time, they were so much happier with married bliss!

"Gosh! These are old photos. We're going back," said Daughter.

Both husband and wife were once filled with delirious joy, as their expressions showed in the photos.

"That's when we were happily married. We were happy together," pointed out Father.

Debra engaged in childhood contemplation, her deep memories. Debra put the photographs in a pile on the table. Her enthusiasm for them was obsessive. The ones of her as a little girl made her deeply sentimental. Debra looked unrecognisable as a sweet little girl, the way she looked (people who saw these photographs had not recognised the girl). The photos showed proud parents with their daughter.

"When did you first meet my mother?"

"I met your mother at school. She was a teenage sweetheart. I fell in love with her. When I was older, I proposed to your mother. We were in love. We got married and settled down. We had a kid," said Father proudly.

"That's me," pointed out Debra.

"We had humble beginnings."

"I am sure you did, back in that time."

Debra stayed in her bedroom. She reflected on every photograph with interested enthusiasm. Debra made an entry in her diary. She kept a diary. She wrote:

Looking at these old photos of my parents was a teenage fascination. A lot has changed since that time. My mother was a teenage bride. A virgin!

With obsessive sentimentality, Debra remembered her past. She had a reminiscence of her parents and when she was only a child!

Chapter 18:

Debra Skives Off School

Debra took the bus to school. She walked a short way to her secondary school. As she reached there, she stayed by the school grounds where some of her form were in groups talking together. They paid attention to Debra, who was quiet while standing close to them. There, the schoolboys had a crush on the stunner. They drooled at the crushingly pretty schoolgirl.

Within minutes, the groups of schoolboys walked away. Waiting at blocks. Debra remained alone with some of her form. The other schoolchildren were present somewhere else, at other blocks, at other entrances.

"Your mum is a whore!" taunted Bridget.

"She isn't a whore. She is my mum," protested Debra.

"What do you bother coming to school? You won't pass."

"I come to school to learn," answered Debra.

Debra felt uneasy at being taunted and teased. In disgust, she walked away, avoiding some members of her form who were intent on taunting, teasing and sneering at her.

Sweet Valentine

Debra felt terribly unhappy and miserable. She was tearful. She felt far too upset. She couldn't face hardly anyone at all, not even her schoolfriends, nor even the bullies, taunters and teasers. She hated them all.

Under the circumstances, Debra had to leave school. In the end, Debra skived off school, getting the bus to go home.

At home, Debra locked herself in her bedroom. Debra cried. She was deeply unhappy. She didn't think of the consequences when she played truant at school. She was relieved to be free. She did regret going to school hours earlier in the morning. Now she disliked school. She dreaded her school days.

Suddenly the telephone rang. Debra did not answer the telephone.

***

Debra attended school the next morning. Her new school uniform was beautiful. She faced her form. She wore her pair of spectacles. Before morning registration, her form tutor called out Debra. Debra acknowledged in response to her name being called out. She got up from her chair and left the table. She came out to the front of the classroom where her form tutor sat at the table.

"Debra, you played truant. Why aren't you going to school, attending your lessons?" asked the form tutor.

"I have had problems recently. My father has left me. I have lost all my jewellery. I can't account for it," blubbered Debra.

"The school has rung your mother. Your mother insists that you go to school without fail," informed the tutor.

"Miss!"

"Not another word. Go and sit down."

Debra obeyed her form tutor. Debra sat down on the chair. She kept silent until the end of registration.

During her periods at school, Debra pretended to work during her lessons. She was too stressed. Debra behaved herself at every lesson. She was on her best behaviour. She was intent on finishing her first day back at school.

She was so relieved at having done it. Debra prepared herself to go to school tomorrow.

Chapter 19:

Valentine Reflection

On a warm day, Debra and Claire sat out in the garden. The two of them confided in each other. At that time they were the only ones at the terraced house.

Earlier, Debra had completed her homework. She, in eager anticipation, was ready to spend time with her close friend. Debra hadn't met Claire since Friday. This Sunday was a quiet and peaceful day. They both came indoors where they continued their conversation. Their reflection on Valentine (a romantic enchantment of thrilling joy. The Valentine's romance of thrills of bewitchment).

"Well? Did you get any Valentine's cards you haven't told me about?" asked Debra.

"Oh! Yes. How about you?"

"I have got a few cards," replied Debra.

"Do you know who your admirers are?"

Debra was excited at the thrill of not knowing her romantic admirers.

"I don't know. It must be Clarage!"

With undoubted certainty, Claire knew her admirer.

"I think I know who sent mine. I romanticised. I dreamt of this Valentine's romance," said Claire dreamily.

With endearment, Debra spoke. She uttered her sweet sentiment.

"My dear sweet! You're romantic. Romantically sweet."

With a pair of scissors, Debra cut off a lock of hair. She gave her lock to Claire.

"Remember me when I am blonde!"

"Oh! I will. Remember me too when I am a spinster, old and grey," implored Claire.

Debra was theatrical. She acted as she recited, moving around the room frantically, captivating Claire's attention. Debra made gestures to her heart, her pounding heart. Claire admired Debra's theatrics. Claire marvelled at her affection, accent and passionate emotion.

Claire engaged in conversation.

"You must go to school. You really must. You'll get in trouble," warned Claire.

Debra spoke in sardonic defiance, then of conversational theatrics.

"I will stay at home and act. Off with my head! Excommunication, thy Lord and Excellency!"

Debra had confidence in acting. After all, she got a part in the last pantomime, a school Christmas production, a full house.

Claire and Debra were in the same set for English Literature. They both read books, from contemporary to classics. They had a passion for reading. (They belonged to a reading group in which they engaged in reading every new title.)

"I really want to pursue a career in acting," said Debra modestly.

Claire underestimated Debra.

"You can act."

"Time will tell," sighed Debra.

Chapter 20:

The Gift

Mr Jenner picked up his daughter. He drove the bewildered passenger to his house where he stayed with his fiancée. This place had become a permanent address of residence.

At the dinner table, Debra and her father and Joanne (her middle name) ate casserole for supper.

Debra at times preferred to stay here rather than at home (her melancholic mother was a depressive!)

Debra felt rather happier at being here. This house was far more cosy and luxurious compared to her house.

"We should be one happy family," said Joanne happily.

"Why don't we?" said Debra.

"How are you feeling?" asked Father.

Debra admitted her condition.

"I am stressed out right now. I am glad to be with you, Dad," grinned Debra.

"How are you doing at school?" asked Father.

"Due to troubles and worries, it has affected me so much. It has affected school."

"Debra, I am sorry if I have caused you problems," apologised Father.

Joanne butted in. "According to your mother, you play truant."

"Bad things have happened to me," moaned Debra.

"Is it that jewellery?" asked Father.

"I am afraid so. I have lost it all. I can't explain the theft," responded Debra.

Joanne took note of Debra's characteristics. "I have noticed you do wear lots of jewellery," said Joanne.

"I have told Debra about it. She won't listen," said Father crossly.

"Having jewellery, it can easily get pinched," said Daughter worriedly.

Debra wondered what's the solution to the problem.

"Don't you think one should put it in a safe?" said Joanne simply.

"They wouldn't know the combination," said Daughter assuredly.

"Quite a good idea. It will be safe in there," pointed out Father.

"Is your jewellery insured?" asked Joanne.

"No, it isn't," blushed Debra.

"That's terrible," said Joanne.

"I have lost everything," sobbed Debra.

Mr Jenner gave his daughter a jewellery case.

"I have got something for you."

Debra did not expect the surprise. Debra took the jewellery case. She opened it. Inside it was a nine-carat gold necklace.

"Dad! Thank you!"

Debra unclasped it. She put the gold necklace around her neck. She fastened it. The thick gold chain glittered around her neck. Debra was delighted with her surprise, her gift. She admired the beautiful gold necklace.

Debra was overwhelmed with delight and joy. Debra, feeling excited, had left the dining table after being excused.

She went to her bedroom, where she stood at the dressing table mirror and admired her gold necklace proudly. Debra marvelled at her gift. She felt much happier, appreciating her father's love and his loving kindness.

Debra took delight in her surprise gift. She was overwhelmed with joy. Debra loved her father even more. Debra wanted to be alone. She took time to reflect on it. She stayed alone in a spare bedroom. She took delight in her lovely necklace, admiring her nine-carat gold necklace.

That night she slept with it around her neck. She took pride in her obsessive possession. Usually, Debra was obsessive about jewellery!

She lost the whole lot!

Debra suffered from melancholy. This time she cheered up.

Debra was pleased with her gift. Debra pleased herself by staying at Spring Vines.

Chapter 21:

A Diary Entry

Debra wrote an entry in her diary:

My father has booked our holiday this year. My father will treat me as a good father does. I will stay at the same hotel as last time. It is a truly romantic place. It's a beautiful hotel with paradise gardens. This hotel has very many rooms and endless corridors. It's so romantic. It has two restaurants. On one night for entertainment, the guitarist plays beautiful guitar music. It's a joy to listen to. I just love the romantic music at night. I am looking forward to sightseeing, as a tourist does. I will marvel at the beautiful scenery, the mountains and the sea. It's such a dream. Seeing and meeting these Spaniards is such a joy. That's what makes my holiday interesting and fascinating. I love the Spanish culture, customs, history, traditions, etiquette, fashion, and food and drink. I remember my last time there, I saw señoritas wearing beautiful red dresses. These female Spaniards are the essence of Spain. Quite remarkable. I remember too last time on my holiday we dined out at restaurants. We went to wine bars and a nightclub. We enjoyed the Spanish nightlife. I also enjoyed the shopping experience too. I learned a little Spanish. A good educational experience learning Spanish. Now I must finish with this entry, of course. The highlight for me of my wonderful holiday, the best thing I remember was when we were on the beautiful sandy beach, the Beach of Dreams, on my very last days there.

I never wanted to leave the beach, ever. I wished I could have stayed there forever till that sunset paradise! All I did there was to keep dreaming and wishing… So ends my dreams!

Chapter 22:

Taunts and Teases

Debra faced animosity from a few of those in her form. They taunted and teased Debra, making fun of her. They sniggered.

Debra ran off back to her form room which was locked. The prefect allowed her in after she explained herself. There she found Claire waiting near the classroom along the corridor, the floor was polished and shiny.

"Will they be together? Won't they be together?" muttered Debra.

"What?" uttered Claire.

"Say you'll be there."

"I'll be there. You shouldn't worry."

"It's the hurt and pain I can't take," groaned Debra.

Claire realised Debra was afraid. Claire stepped forward. Claire put her hand on Debra's shoulder. "I stick up for you, don't I?"

Debra was unappreciative of her friend's protection, her defence.

"You do. It's not enough."

"What do you expect me to do? Fight your battles?"

"I do need you. You're there for me," groaned Debra.

Suddenly, the bell rang. It was time for registration. The form came in and sat down. The form tutor did the registration, calling out the names of the whole form present for registration.

After registration, the form attended their next period. Debra felt pacified from doing Religious Studies. During her lessons, she engaged in religious contemplation. She did not attend her next lesson, instead, she scarpered. She was relieved to get away!

Coming home from school, Debra rested for many hours in her bedroom. She relaxed in comfort. She indulged in luxury.

Later at night, Debra sat in front of the dressing table mirror. She experimented by using different make-up. She used foundation and creams, using various colours, shades and tones which she applied to her face and features. She uglified herself by making herself look unpretty and unlovely. She gained confidence and felt safer. If she got bullied, this time she was prepared for it, ready for action.

***

Going to school, Debra wasn't bullied! Claire protected and defended Debra, as well as the rest of her friends in protective defence.

As usual, Debra attended school. Normally, she was

overworked, exhausted and ingravescent.

In certain subjects, Debra had mixed abilities. Most of the time she was in the top, middle or bottom sets.

Debra felt relieved due to the miraculous changes in her circumstances. She no longer had the threat of being bullied anymore, as bullying had been stamped out of school, and the bullies severely punished, expelled or suspended at times.

Feeling bulimia, Debra did buy an odd dinner ticket from Claire. In some instances, school dinners remained a stigma!

During the course of Debra's school years, it remained a misery. Debra also had some glorious school days!

Debra had a deep fondness for her school teacher. She remembered the school ma'am whom she had loved deeply. In remembrance, she thought of her school teacher deep in her thoughts.

Chapter 23:

Regrets and Disappointments

Debra skived off sports day. That day she stayed at home. She spent the day with Claire. They both were unenthusiastic at taking part in sports day today. They got bored of their uninteresting conversation. They were both uninterested in sports day. (Neither Debra nor Claire was picked for the school team.)

"I have no regrets about not participating in sports day. I am glad to get out of it, of course," said Debra.

"Me too. I am not sporty."

"I like playing rounders, netball and tennis. I am not that good at hockey and athletics."

"Neither am I. I am pleased just to get out of it," sighed Claire.

"The other girls are better than us. They are taking part in sports day," gestured Debra.

Both Debra and Claire were relieved to be together. They enjoyed the comforts of luxuriousness. Claire and Debra are sybarites!

At this time, Debra and Claire were laid-back and carefree. Neither of them missed school whatsoever. They were both relieved to be free, enjoying their time of peace and freedom. They took joy in their good friendship. Their other relationships with boys were a disappointment, a disappointing encounter!

They stayed together all day. It was a joyful pleasure, Debra's invitingness most welcome.

Claire remained unconcerned about school. Claire appreciated Debra's invitation at spending the day with Debra, her best friend.

Epilogue:

PARADISE DREAMS

On the beach of dreams, Debra saw a Spanish boy. She wished he loved her!

She came up to the boy. She showed a romantic interest in the boy, a deep fascination.

Debra had an obsessive love and crush on him. She would not leave him. She stayed as long as she could before leaving.

Looking back she desired him, feeling an exciting thrill!

She ran back to the Spaniard, catching up and reaching him. She smiled at the boy with deep love. The charmed boy smiled back with love. They looked at each other, before walking off past each other again. There they made a trail of footprints in the golden sand.

Chapter 24:

The New Terraced House

Debra lived in a smaller house. The garden was small. Debra felt so humiliated and embarrassed at living in a smaller house, a semi-detached house with a terraced roof.

Debra was unhappy with the changes to her circumstances. She could not live like this. Her life was a misery. Debra blamed her parents for her unhappiness.

Although everything about this house was small, she did in fact have peace, quiet and freedom at last!

Both her parents were divorced. They used to quarrel and argue at times.

Moving into their new house, Mrs Jenner and her daughter unpacked things out of cardboard boxes. They put things away in cupboards and cabinets. The house was cosy and comfortable.

Debra still going to school did suffer from the problems of upheaval.

In the afternoon, Mrs Jenner and Debra took a break. They each ate a sandwich for lunch and drank a mug of tea.

"Blame your father. He owns half of it," glowered

Mother.

"Our standard of living has gone down," remarked Daughter.

"It has. It should be alright. We will get used to it, won't we? We should be happy here. It's our happy home," snarled Mother.

"I like big spaces. I can't get used to it," moaned Debra.

"You will have to. Your father lives in a big house."

"The house is lovely. Joanne is a homemaker. She's house-proud."

Mrs Jenner was maddened at how her ex-husband took advantage of his opportunities.

"Your bloody father. I will kill him," said Mother angrily.

Debra felt irritated by her mother's anger. She got up from the wooden chair. She'd had enough of unpacking. She went to her bedroom. She stayed in her bedroom. She rested on her bed. In depression, Debra sulked. The drastic changes to her life, her circumstances a disappointment and a misery. Her miseries affected her. Suffering from a bout of depression and melancholy.

Debra got used to living here. Fewer and fewer of her friends came to see her at her new home. They had been condescending towards her. With regard to them, she was humiliated by their condescension. Some of her friends did feel alienated by Debra being embarrassed, humiliated and upset. Debra avoided her so-called friends. As a result, they felt alienated from Debra.

For weeks Debra stayed at home. She tried to get used to living here and suburbanise in the new suburban and new area. Debra envied suburbia as well as the middle-class suburbanites.

A few hours later, Debra waited for her friend to come. Claire came on time. Debra showed Claire around her new semi-detached house. Inside the small house, the rooms were furnished and refurbished.

"It's a nice house. You should be happy here," said Claire.

"It's a dolly house, that's what I think of it," said Debra childishly.

Inside the house, Debra's collection of dolls was an amusing attraction and conspicuous sight everywhere around the terraced house, especially on the stairs, landing and sitting room. Debra has a fascination for old dolls.

Since a little girl, she had always had an obsessive tendency to collect dolls. Her possession of dolls an obsessiveness.

Claire was amused at the sight of Debra's dolls everywhere and giggled like a child.

Claire left Debra's house. Debra's whimsical dolls house a Victorian fascination!

Debra's Memories

Debra was subdued in the fifth year. She was rather mournful. Suddenly, she saw something on the noticeboard. She had a flashback. A memory. She remembered the school fete at the institute's quite beautiful gardens.

There she spent time alone with her favourite school teacher whom she adored. She remembered her time of bliss on that hot summer's day. It was an unforgettable summer.

***

That summer term, Debra sat her examinations in the examination hall. The candidates took notice of the invigilator. The candidates passed or failed.

***

The school attendance was far less and less without the school-leavers (and when the fourth years were doing work experience for a fortnight. Every fourth year had been assigned a place).

The pupils, schoolchildren, missed their presence. Their absence made them deeply upset and sad. The school year continues without them.

Debra's Last Time at School (Main Building)

During lunchtime at school, Debra came up to the Music block. Suddenly, she was pulled in by Ann, an artistic schoolgirl.

Debra was pleased to be allowed in the music room. She took delight in her privilege. Debra watched the fifth year schoolgirls playing for the final time. They all played beautifully well altogether. The avant-garde (music group) schoolgirls played the violin, cello, oboe, flute and piano.

They played their instruments well.

These also played for the school orchestra. Debra had watched them perform at the school concert. This was their last performance at school.

Debra was deeply saddened by their final performance. Debra became so upset at watching them perform. Debra was feeling deeply emotional and impassioned. Debra left the music room as soon as they had finished performing.

Debra, feeling too upset, took a chance to skive off school again. She regretted going to school today. Debra had been humiliated, envious and desirous while attending school, watching the schoolgirls perform. Debra had been filled with mixed emotions. She had been prepared to leave school.

***

Terry spent the night at his aunt's house. Debra spent time with her niece. They both shared their experiences and their reflection on school.

Both Debra and Terry were intimate family members. They engaged in a personal conversation.

"How is school?" asked Debra.

"I like school. How about you? How is school?"

"Isn't school about getting a good education as well as getting a qualification? My school life has changed. My school days are worse. It wasn't ever the same ever again. I had memories. It's about my remembrance. Frankly, that's what it's about. I was bereaved. I could not overcome my sorrow and bereavement. I was so sad. I could not hide my sorrow, my disgrace," answered Debra.

"I must say, you're resilient. How did you get over it?"

"My problem was bereavement. I was bereaved, sad and subdued."

"My aunt is miserable," said Niece.

"My mother is traumatised. She has got her problems."

"My aunt is cheerful. How does she cope?"

"She's all we have got in life, so let's not forget. We must cherish it," said Debra earnestly.

They both spent time together talking before leaving to go to bed that summer at midnight.

***

On one examination day, Debra came home from school after she sat her examination. She felt fatigued, knowing she had failed her Biology GCE examination.

A few hours later, she began to dance in her bedroom to dance music (the one previous before that was a school rave tune).

Debra beautifully danced to a dance track. She sang while dancing to the music. She was unaware of neighbours, people, seeing her dancing from the window.

She showed her exposed breasts, braless from a camisole and her legs came out of the slits of her skirt. She was an exhibitionist parading. She had a girlish look of nonchalance, her expressions languished and nonchalant.

Chapter 25:

Days After School Ended

In the summertime, Debra invited Claire to her house. Suddenly, the telephone rang. Debra left her bedroom, leaving Claire alone in her bedroom.

Debra answered the telephone. Meanwhile, Claire took a look at Debra's diary. Claire read an entry:

I am a child of darkness. I stay up at night watching a horror double bill. I go to a Catholic school. I learn Catholic values. I have Catholic morals. I have my own morality. At this institution, Catholicism is the way of life. I may be bad. But how long would it last? Do I fall at the wicked hands of witches! No, my Catholic spirit will ultimately save me. It will pull me out of the fire of Hell. I will believe in God. Maybe I will be converted as a Christian! I don't know my destiny. Am I destined to be a believer?

Debra's mind filled with agitation. Debra was perturbed. Debra went back to her bedroom. Claire, startled, put Debra's personal diary back down on the table. Claire showed Debra her charm bracelet.

"Well, what do you think? Do you like it?

"Why do you go to a Church of England school?" muttered Debra.

"To learn my Christian ways, my religion."

"Well, why don't you put it into practice?" retorted Debra.

"You sanctimonious cow! We have both finished school. It's over!"

"It will be just a memory. It will be just memories," said Debra wistfully.

Both girls stood and looked out of the window dreamily. They admired the view of the back garden. They marvelled at the sight of the small garden which was naturally lovely to one's senses.

A Last Reflection on School

Debra called at Claire's house. She stayed with Claire in the luxurious lounge. They both talked about school. At that time, it was about weeks after leaving school for the final time.

"How do you feel about school being over?" asked Claire.

"I am sad it's over. In some ways I am glad," replied Debra.

"I have left school. I am a school leaver," said Claire assuredly.

Debra thought about the examinations.

"How about your exam results?"

"I have made my decision. I won't be staying on at the Sixth Form. I will go to college."

Debra glanced at her wristwatch. The time was late. It was too late to go home. Debra decided to stay the night at Claire's house. That summer night Debra dreamt of summer bliss. Her euphoria.

Leaving secondary school, Debra walked past hundreds of schoolchildren going down endless paths, their school uniforms amazingly beautiful.

Debra was too proud of her school. She saw their happy facial expressions and the countless schoolboys walking. Every pupil looked greatly beatific. Today was the happiest day of her school life! Her dream of paradise lived on… Her summer dream!

***

So ended Debra's schooldays. Her suffering, miseries and bliss.

- THE END -

*Available worldwide from
Amazon and all good bookstores*

Michael Terence
Publishing

www.mtp.agency

www.facebook.com/mtp.agency

@mtp_agency

www.ingramcontent.com/pod-product-compliance
Lightning Source LLC
LaVergne TN
LVHW011736060526
838200LV00051B/3187